To all who love to look at the night sky
—E.T.

Visit us on the Web! rhcbooks.com

Educators and librarians, for a variety of teaching tools,
visit us at RHTeachersLibrarians.com

Library of Congress Cataloging-in-Publication Data is available upon request.
ISBN 978-0-399-55565-7 (trade) — ISBN 978-0-399-55566-4 (lib. bdg.) — ISBN 978-0-399-55567-1 (ebook)

MANUFACTURED IN CHINA
10 9 8 7 6 5 4 3 2 1   First Edition
Random House Children's Books supports the First Amendment and celebrates the right to read.

Ekaterina Trukhan

Little Fox
and the
Missing Moon

Random House New York

It was a bright day, and little Fox and his friends were busy with spring cleaning and sprucing up their homes.

Fox dusted off his books and polished his Detecting Magnifying Glass until it sparkled.
He wanted to be ready for the next mystery.

At bedtime, Fox made some
hot chocolate and got into
bed with a new mystery book.

He was tired after
such a long, busy day.
As soon as the moon
appeared in his window,
he fell asleep.

But he had a very bad dream!
He dreamed that monsters
had eaten the moon!

The strange dream woke Fox up in the middle of the night. He jumped out of bed and looked out the window. The moon was gone!

Oh, no!

Fox had to find the missing moon.
But he was going to need help from
his friends to solve such a puzzling
case. So he grabbed his flashlight
and headed into the night.

Fox made his way through the dark, dark woods. As a detective, he wasn't *too* afraid of the strange noises and big eyes that peeked out at him.

Hello? Who's there?
I'm not scared of you,
horrible monsters!

Hello, Fox! It's your friends Owl, Wolf, and Bear. We're looking for the lost moon and want your help.

Oh! I didn't recognize you in the darkness. Let's get Rabbit, and together we'll find the moon!

As the friends approached Rabbit's house, they saw a bright light coming from the window. The door was open, so they went inside.

There was Rabbit, washing something
in the sink. He was so busy that he
didn't notice his guests.

The friends came closer and closer.
They saw something floating in the
sink. . . . It was the moon!

I took the moon down to wash off the dirt. Look at how it shines!

But now I have to put it back.

Owl, Wolf, Bear, and Fox helped Rabbit put the moon back in the sky. The clean moon was more beautiful and bright than ever.

The mystery of the lost moon
was solved, and Fox went home.
He planned to go back to bed to
dream about a new case.

But first he looked out the
window to check on the moon.